MISSING!

Flame

Have you seen this kitten?

He is a magic kitten of royal blood, missing from his own world.
His uncle, Ebony, is very keen that he is found quickly.
Flame may be hard to spot as he often appears in a
variety of fluffy kitten colours but you can recognize him
by his big emerald eyes and whiskers that crackle with magic!

He is believed to be looking for a young friend to take care of him.

...let Ebony,

Sue Bentley's books for children often include animals or fairies. She lives in Northampton and enjoys reading, going to the cinema, and sitting watching the frogs and newts in her garden pond. If she hadn't been a writer, she would probably have been a skydiver or brain surgeon. The main reason she writes is that she can drink pots and pots of tea while she's typing. She has met and owned many cats, and each one has brought a special sort of magic to her life.

Magic Kitten

Double Trouble

SUE BENTLEY

Illustrated by Angela Swan

PUFFIN

PUFFIN BOOKS

UK | USA | Canada | Ireland | Australia
India | New Zealand | South Africa

Puffin Books is part of the Penguin Random House group of companies
whose addresses can be found at global.penguinrandomhouse.com.

puffinbooks.com

First published 2006
This edition published 2016
001

Text copyright © Sue Bentley, 2006
Illustrations copyright © Angela Swan, 2006

Set in Bembo 15pt/22pt
Printed in Great Britain by Clays Ltd, St Ives plc

A CIP catalogue record for this book is available from the British Library

ISBN: 978-0-141-36779-8

www.greenpenguin.co.uk

MIX
Paper from
responsible sources
FSC® C018179

Penguin Random House is committed to a
sustainable future for our business, our readers
and our planet. This book is made from Forest
Stewardship Council® certified paper.

To Poppy – sweetest tabby girl

★Prologue★

'Uncle Ebony!' gasped the young white
lion, leaping behind a huge rock just as
the shadow of an enormous adult lion
fell across him. There was a dazzling
white flash and a burst of silver
sparkles. Where the young white lion
had been now crouched a tiny silver
tabby kitten.

Flame's tiny kitten heart beat fast as

his uncle passed close by where he hid.
He could hear Ebony's angry roar and
imagined his fierce, ice-cold eyes.

'Flame must be found and then he
will die!' Ebony hissed aloud.

Suddenly a huge paw, almost as
large as the kitten's entire body,
reached round the rock. Flame laid his
tiny ears flat and bit back a whimper
as he was scooped up. This was it. He
was dead.

But instead of being dragged out on
to the sand, he found himself being
swept further back into the safety of
the rocks. An old grey lion looked
down at him.

'Cirrus! Thank you,' Flame mewed
gratefully.

Cirrus bowed respectfully. 'I am glad

to see you again, Prince Flame. But it
is not safe for you to stay.'

Flame lifted his chin. 'I must regain
the Lion Throne!'

Cirrus's kindly hot breath ruffled the
kitten's fuzzy fur. 'True. But first you
must grow strong and wise. Your uncle
is powerful and heartless and he has
many spies. Stay in your disguise and
hide far from here.'

Flame's big emerald eyes sparked with
anger. 'I will, but only until my powers
are stronger. Then Ebony's rule will
end!'

Cirrus smiled with pride and
affection. 'May that day come soon. Go
now, Prince Flame. Go . . .'

Flame felt the power building within
him. Sparks ignited in his silver tabby

fur and his whiskers crackled. He gave a tiny mew of alarm as he felt himself falling. Falling . . .

★ Chapter ★
ONE

'Mia's here. I'll let her in!' Kim Taylor called excitedly to her mum, who was putting sheets on the spare bed.

Kim dashed down the stairs two at a time. It had been a year since she last saw her cousin.

Mia's parents were both musicians. They took turns in living in the houses they owned in France and Italy. Now

Mia was staying for a week during the spring holiday, so there would be loads of time to catch up and do exciting things. Kim couldn't wait.

As she opened the front door, Kim beamed at the young girl standing in front of her.

Mia was tall with short, feathery, blonde hair. She was wearing expensive-looking clothes and trainers and held a glittery pink backpack that dangled by its straps.

'Your hair looks cool!' Kim said, leaning forward to give Mia a hug. 'I'm so glad you're here. We're going to have a great time!'

Mia pulled away from Kim looking awkward. 'Yeah, well, that's what Mum and Dad said and I didn't believe *them*

either. They don't care if I die of
boredom as long as I'm out of the way
while they go off and do a tour of
nightclubs with their stupid old band!'
She rolled her eyes and sighed
dramatically. 'Anyway, I'm here now.'

'Excuse me, you two!'

Mia and Kim stood back as her dad
staggered in with two enormous suitcases
which he had brought in from the car.

'Are you staying for a whole year, love?' he joked to Mia, who looked horrified at the thought.

Kim felt awful. She thought Mia had really wanted to come to their house for the holiday. She wasn't sure what to say.

'Miaow-row!'

Kim looked down. The complaining noise came from a smart, plastic pet carrier at Mia's feet, which she hadn't seen to begin with.

'All right, Bibi. You can come out in a minute,' Mia said.

Kim crouched by the carrier to look inside. All she could see was a mass of fluffy cream fur and big round eyes. 'What sort of cat is she?' she asked excitedly.

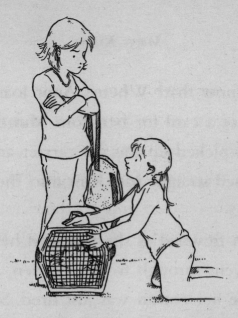

'A pedigree Persian,' Mia said proudly.
'Mum and Dad bought her for me
before they went on tour. Bibi cost
loads of money and she's won heaps of
rosettes and cups at cat shows. Her full
name is Beautiful Lady of Bromford
Farm.'

'That's a long name. No wonder you
call her Bibi!' Kim said.

Mia put her hands on her hips. 'All
pedigree cats have long names. Don't

you know that? Where's Aunt Joan? I've got a card for her from Mum.'

Mia picked up the pet carrier and marched straight past Kim into the house.

Kim frowned as she followed her in and went through to the kitchen. Maybe her cousin was just tired. She knew that could make people bad-tempered and sulky.

Mia sat at the pine table. Mrs Taylor was just giving her a glass of orange juice.

'Thanks, Aunt Joan. And thanks for letting me come and stay,' Mia said sweetly.

'You're welcome, Mia,' Mrs Taylor said. 'Kim's been dying to spend some time with you. You know, you two were very close when you were small.'

Mia gave Kim a long look. Kim thought she saw a ghost of a smile cross Mia's face, but it was gone before she could smile back.

'Miaw-wow-wow!' Another loud wail of protest came from the pet carrier.

'It sounds like poor Bibi's fed up with being shut in there. Shall I let her out or do you want to do it, Mia?' Kim asked helpfully.

'No. You can do it, Kim,' Mia said.

'Hello, girl. Don't be nervous,' Kim said gently, kneeling down to open the catch. She was dying to see what a champion, prize-winning Persian looked like.

A huge fluffy cream cat came out slowly into the room. Bibi backed up against the fridge and gazed around the kitchen with big orange eyes. She had a flat face, with a wrinkled forehead and a tiny snub nose.

'Do you want to make friends?' Kim rubbed her fingertips together and made a friendly noise.

Bibi opened her mouth and hissed loudly. Suddenly, she dashed round behind Kim.

'Ow-oww!' Kim yelled in pain as sharp claws dug into her leg through her jeans. She straightened up and waggled her leg, trying to shake Bibi off. 'Help, Mia! Call her off!' she shouted.

Mia just started laughing. 'You should see yourself!'

Kim's mum acted quickly. She filled a

small glass with water and threw it over the angry cat. Bibi gave a yowl, let go of Kim's ankle and ran under the table.

'Hey!' Mia ducked down to scoop up her pet. 'Did that nasty lady throw water on you?' she soothed, stroking Bibi's wet fur.

'Are you all right, Kim?' asked her mum.

Kim nodded shakily. She rolled up her jeans and examined her leg. There were two long scratches. They stung like mad, but luckily they didn't look very deep.

'Oh, don't be such a baby, Kim!' Mia said.

'Cat scratches can be really sore, Mia,' Mrs Taylor said with a frown. 'Does Bibi often act like that? You may have to keep her shut in your room if she's going to attack people.'

Mia rose from the chair with Bibi under one arm. There was a hurt look in her big blue eyes. 'Bibi was only playing. She was being friendly. I'd like to see my room now, please.'

'You go on up. It's the room to the right that faces the front garden. Kim will come up in a minute.' Mrs Taylor turned to her daughter. 'We'd better clean up those scratches first.'

As her mum fetched some antiseptic, Kim heard Mia sniff loudly as she stomped upstairs. Kim rested her leg on a chair while her mum cleaned the scratches.

'There. You'll do,' her mum said a few minutes later, putting the cap back on a tube of cream. 'Ready to go up and help Mia unpack?'

'Do I have to?' Kim asked reluctantly. She didn't feel much like being nice to Mia at the moment.

'Come on now. Mia's our guest. She's probably missing her parents and feeling lonely.' Mrs Taylor gave her daughter's thick brown ponytail a gentle tug. 'Let's try and make her feel welcome.'

'I'll try,' Kim promised as she got to her feet and went upstairs to find Mia. But she had a sinking feeling in her tummy. She didn't think having her cousin to stay was going to turn out like she had expected at all.

★Chapter★
TWO

After supper on the patio, Kim took Mia and Bibi into the garden. Luckily Bibi was more interested in exploring the flower beds than clawing people's legs.

'Don't go eating slugs or snails or you'll be sick later,' Mia said to Bibi.

If she is, I'm not clearing it up, Kim thought. She glanced down the narrow lawn, with its old apple tree at the bottom, to where her dad was stacking old flowerpots and seed trays outside his shed. He saw her looking and beckoned excitedly for her to come down.

Mia had seen him too. 'Why's he waving about like that?'

'I don't know,' Kim said, walking down the lawn to find out.

Mia followed her. 'I'm coming too.'

As Kim and Mia drew close, Mr Taylor pointed inside the shed and put a finger to his lips. 'Shhh! Be very quiet,' he whispered. 'See that cracked flowerpot? There's a robin's nest inside it.'

'Really?' Kim leaned forward slowly. She saw the nest of woven grass and leaves. Then she spotted five little fuzzy heads, all with their eyes closed. 'Oh! It's got five chicks in it!' she breathed.

'Let me see.' Mia pushed past Kim rudely. But when she saw the chicks, her face softened. 'Aah! They are so sweet! Look how they're all snuggled up together. But how did the robins get into the shed?'

Kim's dad pointed to a small hole in the wall, up near the roof. 'But it beats me why they chose that hole, when there was an easier way in,' he said. He showed them the stone that had been propping the door shut. Even with the door closed, there was a gap at the top.

'Da–ad!' Kim scolded with a grin. 'Haven't you mended that broken catch yet?'

Mr Taylor pretended to look hurt. 'All in good time.'

Kim gave him a playful shove. He'd been saying that for months!

Mia was fascinated by the fluffy brown chicks. She seemed genuinely relaxed and happy for the first time since she arrived. It gave Kim an idea.

'Come with me,' she said, tugging at Mia's arm.

Mia frowned suspiciously. 'Why? Where are we going?'

'Da-dah!' Kim opened the bedroom cupboard to reveal her new telescope in all its glory. 'Gran and Granddad Taylor bought it for my tenth birthday, this year. I haven't used it much yet.'

'Not bad,' Mia said, trying not to look too impressed.

'I know. Gran and Granddad are great. They never buy boring stuff like slippers and bumper packs of felt-tip pens,' Kim said, lifting out the telescope. 'I thought we could watch the robins going in and out of the shed to feed their chicks.'

Mia nodded. 'I'll help you set it up.'

They moved a small bedside table in front of the window. After Kim had put the telescope on its stand, she explained how to focus it and then stood back to let Mia have the first look.

'I can see a robin on the apple tree!' Mia said excitedly. 'Its beak's full of grubs or something. Now it's flown into the shed!'

Kim and Mia took turns to watch the robins coming and going. They brought all sorts of food. Sometimes it was small caterpillars or grubs and once it was a juicy wriggling worm.

Mia really loved the telescope. She couldn't stop looking through it. 'I can see the farm on the hill at the end of your garden.'

Kim felt pleased that Mia was taking

an interest in something at last. Her cousin even smiled a couple of times.

'Having a good time, you two?' Mr Taylor popped his head round the door. He held up a dusty green bag. 'Look what else I found in the shed!'

Kim leapt on it eagerly. 'That's my old tent! I haven't seen it for ages. We could camp out in the garden tonight. Can we, Dad?'

Her dad smiled. 'I don't see why not. It's a warm night. If you can drag yourselves away from those robins for ten seconds, I'll help you put up the tent.'

By the time Kim and Mia were spreading groundsheets and sleeping bags inside the tent, the sky was a deep blue and stars were glinting above the apple tree.

'It'll be fun camping out, won't it, Mia?' Kim said.

But suddenly Mia seemed to have second thoughts. 'Actually I might not bother. It's going to be cold and draughty in that old tent.' She stood up. 'I'm going inside to feed Bibi. I'll let you know what I decide later,' she said.

Kim's spirits sank. Just when they
seemed to be getting on all right, Mia
had gone all sulky again. She sighed
and decided to go down to the shed
for a last check on the robin's nest. Her
dad had put the stone back in front of
the door. She moved it aside very
carefully and peered in. The chicks
were sleeping, safe and warm.

She was putting the stone back
when, from the corner of her eye, she
noticed a faint glow. Edging round the
side of the shed, she went to
investigate.

'Oh!' Kim gasped.

There, half hidden by tall weeds,
crouched a cute silver tabby kitten. It
blinked up at her with big, scared,
green eyes. Kim looked closer. Its fur

26

seemed to be glittering with hundreds of silver sparks, like tiny Christmas tree lights.

Kim shook her head in confusion. Of course its fur couldn't be glowing, and when she looked again the sparkles did seem to have gone.

But what was it doing here? Had someone abandoned it?

'Hello, little puss,' she said in a soft, gentle voice, bending down so she wouldn't frighten the kitten, who was trembling all over. 'Don't be scared. I won't hurt you. I wonder where you came from.'

The kitten lifted its tiny head. As it peered through the tangled leaves some of the fear seemed to fade from its emerald eyes. 'I have run away. My uncle is searching for me. He wants to kill me,' it mewed softly.

Kim's jaw dropped in complete shock. She lost her balance and almost tumbled sideways.

The kitten had just answered her!

★Chapter★
THREE

Kim knelt in the patch of weeds and stared at the silver tabby kitten in complete amazement.

'Did . . . did you just say something?' she stuttered. 'What's going on? Is this a trick?'

Kim looked round her wildly to see if anyone else was there. Maybe Mia was playing a trick on her. She seemed to enjoy thinking up new ways of being mean.

The kitten twitched its tiny tail. 'This is no trick. I am Prince Flame. Who are you?'

'I'm Kim. Kim Taylor,' she answered. 'Why is your uncle trying to kill you? And why are you here?'

'My Uncle Ebony has taken the Lion Throne to which I am heir. He will do all he can to stop me reclaiming what is mine!' Flame rumbled softly, with a flash of anger in his emerald eyes.

Kim looked down at the tiny, fluffy kitten, which seemed even smaller against the tall weeds. 'No offence, but you don't exactly look as if you're a prince,' she said.

'I will show you!' The kitten sat up indignantly.

There was a silver flash, so bright that Kim had to look away. When she looked back, the kitten was gone and in its place stood a huge, majestic, young white lion with glowing emerald eyes. 'Do not be afraid,' he said in a deep velvety growl.

Kim took a deep breath and tried very hard to stay calm. 'OK! Flame. I . . . I believe you!' she stammered.

With another blinding flash, the tiny silver tabby kitten reappeared. 'I need to hide from my enemies, Kim. That is why I am here. Can you help me?'

Despite the shock of having been faced with a lion prince in his true form, Kim's soft heart melted. Right now, Flame was just a frightened little kitten.

'I'll look after you, don't worry.' She bent down quickly and picked Flame up. Her fingers tingled faintly as his fur sparkled, and as the sparks faded they left a warm glow in her hands. 'You can come and live with me! My parents won't mind. We sometimes foster cats and kittens for the local pet centre.'

Flame reached up two paws and rested them on her chest. 'You must tell no one, Kim,' he purred, with a serious look in his eyes.

'You'll be my secret,' she promised, cuddling his little body.

Kim was determined to look after Flame and keep him safe. He was so gorgeous that she loved him already. Even Mia's meanness wasn't going to ruin this holiday now.

She carried him towards the open kitchen door, where her mum was preparing hot drinks and Bibi was licking her dish clean of cat food. Just then, Mia came into the kitchen and saw Kim. 'Where did you get that kitten?' she asked in surprise.

'I found him behind the shed,' Kim replied. She turned to her mum. 'Flame must be a stray. He seems hungry and scared. I'm going to feed him and then I'll make a bed for him in my bedroom. That's OK, isn't it?'

Her mum smiled. 'It looks like you've already made your mind up. I like his name.' She stroked Flame's head. 'He's adorable, isn't he? Just don't get too fond of him, in case someone claims him. I'll go and phone the pet centre and say we have him, in case someone reports a lost kitten.'

'OK, Mum, thanks,' Kim said. She felt pretty sure that no one was going to claim this particular kitten!

While her mum went out to use the phone, Kim took a spare dish from a cupboard. She filled it with cat food, and set in on the floor some distance away from Bibi. 'There you are, Flame.'

Flame scampered over to the dish and started munching.

Bibi stopped licking her lips and froze as she seemed to notice Flame for the first time. She pinned her ears back and glared.

Kim recognized the warning signs

and took a step forward, ready to grab Bibi. Mia just smirked as she looked on.

But Kim was too late. Bibi charged straight at Flame and wopped him across the head with her big front paw.

'Yow-owl!' Flame went bowling across the floor and the cat food flew everywhere. He skidded to a halt against the table leg. Scrambling to his feet, Flame gave himself a shake and turned to face Bibi.

Kim saw big sparkles fizzing all over his silver tabby fur, his whiskers crackled and his eyes glowed like green coals.

She felt a weird prickling sensation down her spine.

Flame lifted a paw and sparks sprayed out towards the angry Persian.

Bibi went stiff all over. Her paws pointed downwards and her tail stuck up as straight as a broomstick. She jerked as if trying to run away and started bouncing across the kitchen on tiptoes.

'Eeek!' she squeaked loudly, her orange eyes rolling round and round as she bobbed up and down like a clockwork toy. 'Eeek! Eeek!'

Mia, who didn't seem to have seen the sparks fly from Flame, stared in horror at her pet. 'What's wrong with her? Why's she squeaking like a mouse?'

Kim bent down to check that Flame was all right. He nudged her hand with the top of his head to let her know he was fine. 'Bibi can't be like that for much longer or Mum will call the vet and there'll be an awful fuss,' Kim whispered to him urgently.

Flame frowned, but pointed a tabby paw, so that one big silver spark shot out and hit Bibi on the nose.

Bibi stopped suddenly. The big Persian flopped on to the floor and lay there blinking in surprise at Flame.

Mia rushed over to her. She examined her pet and frowned. 'She seems fine now, but she must have had some kind of jealous fit. Pedigrees are very highly strung, you know! It's because of Flame. She doesn't like him. You'll have to get rid of that kitten, Kim. It's only a scrappy little stray anyway!'

Kim felt herself getting cross. 'Highly strung? Bibi's just a spiteful posh fleabag! I don't care if she's got a pedigree as long as my arm! And Flame's a lot more than a stray. He's m . . .' She only just managed to stop

herself in time. 'He's mine!' She had
been about to say 'magic'. She was
going to have to be a lot more careful
about keeping Flame's secret. 'Anyway,
Mum said Flame could stay and that's
final!' she tailed off.

Mia rounded on Kim. 'You can't talk
to me like that!' she fumed.

Just then Mrs Taylor came back into
the kitchen. 'What's all this about?' she
wanted to know.

Kim and Mia began talking at once.

After a second or two, Mrs Taylor
held up her hand for silence. 'That's
enough, both of you. Bibi seems fine
now, Mia. Why don't you take her for
a walk in the garden and calm down?
Kim, you'd better feed Flame.'

Mia tossed her head and glared at

Kim. 'All right. Come on, Bibi.'

Bibi sidled past Flame and gave a half-hearted hiss as she dashed after Mia.

Kim cleared up the spilt cat food and then set more out for Flame. He went straight to the food and began eating, purring loudly in contentment.

Kim felt a bit guilty for giving in to her temper and shouting at Mia. Maybe she'd try and make up with her later. She went and gave her mum a hug to make herself feel better. 'Thanks for letting Flame stay, Mum.'

'Hmm. I might have been too hasty about that,' her mum said. 'If Bibi's going to bully Flame, maybe it would be better if we found another place for him to stay.'

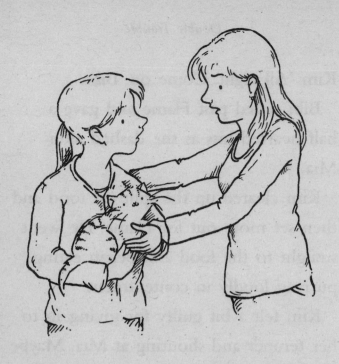

'No!' Kim burst out. 'I'll make sure I keep an eye on them both. Please, Mum. Flame chose me for his friend and I've promised him – er, I mean I've promised myself – that I'm going to keep him safe.'

Her mum smiled. 'OK. I just hope there's no more trouble between those cats.'

'There won't be!' Kim declared. *I'd bet a week's pocket money that Bibi's learned her lesson*, she thought.

★Chapter★
FOUR

Kim poured hot chocolate into a flask, put crisps and biscuits on to a tray, and tucked a couple of torches under her arm before heading for the garden. 'Come on, Flame.'

As she and Flame reached the tent Mia and Bibi came up the garden towards her. When Bibi spotted Flame she stopped dead and then walked

round him very slowly, making a big
circle of space.

In cat language, Kim reckoned that
meant, 'I'm not going to give you any
more trouble.'

There was an awkward silence.

'Have you been exploring?' Kim
asked Mia in a friendly voice, still
feeling a bit guilty about earlier.

'Yes. We went to see the sheep in the
field that joins on to your garden,' Mia
said in a subdued voice. She glanced
down at Flame. 'He's pretty cute for an
ordinary moggy, isn't he? I hope Bibi
didn't hurt him.'

It seemed that Mia was willing to
make amends too.

'Don't worry. Flame's fine,' Kim
assured her. She was pleased they were

talking again but wondered what Mia
would say if she knew that Flame was a
royal prince! 'Is Bibi OK?'

'Yes, thanks,' Mia said. 'Er . . . Are
those chocolate-chip cookies? They're
my favourite.'

'Help yourself. We've got loads.' Kim
smiled and this time Mia smiled back.

It was dark inside the tent now, so
they ate by torchlight. Bibi curled up
on Mia's sleeping bag, still keeping a
watchful eye on Flame.

When the food and drink were
finished, Kim tucked Flame in beside
her. He yawned and curled up close. 'I
feel safe here, Kim. Thank you,' he
mewed softly, so that only Kim could
hear.

Kim stroked the top of his silky

head. She loved having Flame with her.

Mia also lay down and closed her eyes. 'Goodnight, Kim.'

'Goodnight, Mia,' Kim said as she turned off the torch. She snuggled down into the sleeping bag. 'Sweet dreams, Flame,' she whispered.

She felt him touch her chin lightly with the tip of his little cold nose.

Kim woke up with a start. It was still pitch-dark. Someone was shaking her arm urgently.

'Mia?' she said sleepily. 'What's wrong?'

'There's something outside the tent!' Mia whispered hoarsely. 'Listen! Can't you hear it?'

Kim listened hard. At first all was quiet and she thought Mia must be imagining things. Then there was a rustling noise and the tent's walls shook as something brushed against it.

Kim caught her breath. There *was* something out there!

Beside her, Flame gave a low growl.

'What is it?' Mia said faintly.

Kim's fingers trembled as she felt about in the darkness for the torch. She switched it on and the beam wobbled all over the place as she pointed the torch at the tent flap.

Suddenly a long, bony head pushed inside the tent. It had no hair and pale staring eyes. A low mournful cry came from it.

'Aargh!' Mia screeched. 'It's an alien!'

'No, it's not. It's only a sheep!' Kim said, relieved. 'You must have left the field gate open, Mia, and they've wandered into the garden.'

But Mia didn't seem to hear and only screamed even louder. Now Bibi joined in and started to howl. The sheep with its head inside the tent bleated in terror and rolled its eyes in fright, before hurriedly backing out.

The noise everyone was making was deafening. Kim groaned. The whole street was going to wake up at any minute.

She took a deep breath and yelled, 'SHUT UP!'

Mia stopped screaming abruptly and looked hurt. 'There's no need to shout!'

But Kim was already crawling towards the tent flap. She stuck her head outside. There were at least twenty big white sheep in the garden, munching on flowers, lettuces and young carrot tops in her dad's prized vegetable patch. Her dad was usually really easy-going, but he was dead strict about keeping the field gate closed.

'When Dad sees this, he's going to go bananas!' Kim shuffled back inside the tent. The only sign of Mia was a big lump halfway down the sleeping bag. Kim shook it urgently. 'Mia! Come on. Get up!'

'Leave me alone!' said a muffled voice.

'Look, I'm really sorry I shouted at you,' Kim said. She felt desperate. 'You've got to help get those sheep back into the field or I'm in for a severe telling-off!'

'Tough!' Mia said stubbornly.

Kim didn't waste any more time. 'I'll just have to do it by myself then,' she whispered to Flame as she crawled out of the tent.

'I will help,' he mewed beside her.

Kim ran towards the nearest sheep. 'Shooo!' she whispered, flapping her arms at it. But instead of heading towards the field, it ran in circles. The other sheep started running in all directions. Kim threw up her hands in despair. 'I'm never going to get the silly things back in.'

But just then, from the corner of her eye, Kim saw Flame run forward, his coat glowing with silver sparks and his whiskers crackling with electricity. A cloud of tiny silver sparks rose into the air and fell on the sheep like gentle glittery rain.

Kim watched in amazement as each one of them began to swell. They grew fatter and fatter, until they turned into surprised-looking woolly balloons that floated a few centimetres off the ground!

Kim tapped one of them gently and it began drifting down the garden towards the field. Gaining confidence, she ran to each one of them in turn. Soon all the sheep-balloons were floating down the garden and heading back over the fence.

Kim watched them sink gently down to the grass and turn back into normal-looking sheep.

'Phew! Thanks, Flame!' she said as
she latched the gate.

'You are welcome!' Flame gave her a
whiskery grin.

'What's all this noise about?' Kim's
dad came running down the lawn in his
nightclothes. His hair was all messed up
and he looked sleepy-eyed and grumpy.

'Er . . . it was only a couple of sheep
in the garden,' Kim said hurriedly. 'One

of them stuck its head in the tent. It was quite funny really. Mia thought it was an alien . . .' She stopped as her cousin crawled out of the tent with a face like thunder.

Mia ran straight up to Kim's dad. 'Oh, Uncle Brian! Kim's been so horrible. I was really scared, but she didn't care. She just yelled at me. It's not my fault *she* left the gate open!'

'But, that's not true . . .' Kim gaped at Mia in shock. 'I mean, I did shout at her, but . . .'

Mr Taylor held up his hand for silence. 'I've told you a hundred times about leaving that gate open. It was up to you to check it. Mia's a guest, so she can't be expected to know the house rules.'

'Yes, I know. But . . .' Kim burst out.

'That's enough, Kimberley,' her dad said sternly. 'Next time you lose your temper, try counting to ten, OK?'

Her dad only used her full name when he was about to explode. Kim gave up.

'I think it's best if you both spend the rest of the night indoors,' Mr Taylor decided.

Kim and Mia trudged into the house behind him. Kim didn't trust herself to speak to Mia. She went straight up to her bedroom and flung herself on her bed. Flame jumped up next to her.

'It's not fair!' Kim fumed. It didn't seem to matter how hard she tried to get on with her cousin, they just kept falling out!

Flame licked her hand with his rough

little tongue. 'Don't feel sad,' he mewed.

As Kim stroked his soft fur she started to feel a little bit better. 'I'm so glad you're here, Flame. You're a real friend.'

★Chapter★
FIVE

Kim stared glumly down at her egg on toast. She had dreamed of floating sheep, chasing her down a long winding path. All of them had Mia's face.

Flame was eating a dish of cat food.

'Have you and Mia made any plans for today?' her mum asked.

She shook her head. Mia had asked

for breakfast in bed as a special treat.
Kim hadn't spoken to her yet. Mia was
probably still sulking.

Kim's mum poured herself a cup of
tea. 'Why don't you two cycle over to
see your grandparents?' she suggested.
'You know how you love going over
there. Mia might enjoy it too.'

Mike and Ruth Taylor, Kim's dad's parents, lived in a rambling, red-brick house that backed on to the river. They'd recently bought the *Sally Ann*, an old houseboat, and were enjoying doing it up.

Kim felt herself warming to the idea of going to visit them. 'Mia could ride my old bike and we could put Flame and Bibi in the baskets. I'll go and phone Gran and tell her we're coming.'

Her mum looked pleased. 'Tell Gran we'll come along later. We'll bring a picnic with us.'

Flame lifted his head to sniff at all the delicious smells of spring as Kim and Mia cycled along. They passed trees heavy with pink and white blossom.

Mia seemed to have cheered up a bit and on the way Kim told her about the *Sally Ann*.

'I love boats,' Mia said. 'One of Dad's friends has got a fantastic yacht. We sometimes go for a cruise on it.'

They turned into an avenue where primroses dotted the grass verges. Kim saw a figure come out of a large, red-brick house. She waved. 'Gran!'

'Hello, you two!' Ruth Taylor smiled as Kim and Mia drew up. They dismounted and wheeled their bikes through the garden gate.

Kim took Flame out of the basket and went to give her gran a hug. 'Hi, Gran. This is Flame.'

'Hello, love.' Her gran returned the hug and stroked Flame. 'What a gorgeous little kitten!'

Flame purred loudly.

'Hello, Mia. It's lovely to see you too,' Mrs Taylor said. 'And this must be Bibi. She's a champion, isn't she?'

'Yes, she is,' Mia said, looking pleased.

'Where's Granddad?' Kim asked.

'I'll give you one guess!' her gran said.

'Working on the boat?' Kim said with a grin.

Mrs Taylor took them into the back
garden and through a private gated
wood. The path came out at the
riverbank. Kim could hear the faint
sound of rushing water from the steep
weir in the distance.

There was an old houseboat, with
peeling red and white paint, moored to
a small wooden jetty. The name *Sally
Ann* was painted on her bow.

Mike Taylor was on the deck. He wiped his hand on his overalls and waved an oily rag in the air like a flag. 'Ahoy there!' he called.

'Is that their boat? What an old heap!' Mia said in a piercing whisper.

'It's got a stove and a bed and everything inside. I love it,' Kim said, feeling embarrassed by her cousin's rudeness.

But Gran just winked at Kim. 'So do we! Come and have a look. Mind your head, Mia.'

Kim ducked and went into the cabin. Gran and Granddad had been hard at work. It smelt of fresh paint and brass polish. There were new lace curtains at the windows and cheerful knitted cushions on the chairs. Even Mia was fascinated by the way the table and bed folded away.

Flame went straight over and curled up on a cushion.

Kim smiled. Anyone would think he'd lived on a houseboat all his life!

'I was just about to plant up some window boxes before you arrived,' Mrs Taylor said. 'Would you like to help?'

'We'd love to, wouldn't we, Mia?' Kim said.

'I don't mind,' Mia agreed.

Gran fetched some compost and trays of plants and they got to work.

About ten minutes later, Mia sat back and dusted compost off her hands. 'I'm bored now. I want to do something else,' she declared.

'Why don't you go and have a look

round,' Mrs Taylor suggested. 'The woods are pretty at this time of year.'

'OK. See you later,' Mia called as she wandered away with Bibi trotting at her heels.

Kim helped Gran finish planting the rest of the marigolds and petunias and then stood back to admire the window boxes. 'These will look a picture in a few weeks' time,' Gran said.

'Hello! Anyone ready for a picnic?' called a voice.

Kim's mum and dad had arrived. They carried two baskets that were bursting with delicious food and drink.

'Now you're talking!' said Granddad, coming out of the cabin. 'I'll just go and get cleaned up.'

Kim, Flame, her parents and

grandparents trooped through the gate
to the woods back towards the house.

'Where's Mia?' Kim peered through
the trees.

'She can't have gone far,' Gran said.
'The path only leads to our garden. If
Mia had come back to the river, we'd
have seen her.'

'Maybe she went into the house,'
Kim's mum suggested. But after a
search of the house and garden there
was still no sign of Mia or Bibi.

Kim had a sudden thought. 'I bet she's hiding in the woods, waiting for us to come and find her! Flame and I will go and have a look.'

Kim had walked a little way into the woods when Flame pricked up his ears and gave a worried little mew.

'What's wrong, Flame?' Kim stopped walking and listened hard. A faint scream floated towards her on the breeze. It was coming from the direction of the river. 'That sounds like Mia!'

Kim ran forward. She caught a sudden glimpse through the trees of a red and white boat drifting past. It was the *Sally Ann*. She must have slipped her mooring!

As Kim drew nearer, she saw a movement at one of the cabin windows. She spotted a small, white-faced figure clutching a large cream cat.

★Chapter★
SIX

'The weir!' Kim remembered with a thrill of horror. The *Sally Ann* would be swept over. 'We have to do something, Flame!'

She hurtled towards the edge of the woods. Flame bounded along beside her, his coat alive with sparks and his whiskers crackling.

Kim's whole body suddenly filled

with a hot swirly feeling. A flash of energy shot up her spine. She felt her arms stretch out and her muscles tense as she jumped up – and soared straight into the air!

Strong wings carried her upwards. Her body had become powerful but light and covered with smooth brown feathers.

Flame had turned her into a hawk!

There was a rush of wind against Kim's face as the countryside fell away with dizzying speed. She flapped her wings and flew towards the *Sally Ann*. Far below, she spotted a small motor boat making its way towards the houseboat. Someone else on the river must have spotted the drifting *Sally Ann* and, realizing the danger, given chase.

But would the motor boat reach the *Sally Ann* in time? She was drifting faster now and the rushing sound of the weir was getting louder.

With her keen bird's sight, Kim saw the *Sally Ann*'s mooring rope trailing out behind her in the water. She swooped down to the river and grasped the wet rope in her clawed feet. It was heavy and hard to lift, but she held on tightly, determined not to drop it.

Kim flew upwards slowly, her feet

and wings aching, and struck out for the rescue boat.

Gasping for breath, Kim hovered above the rescue boat and dropped the rope on to the deck. The boat's owner quickly ran forward. He grabbed the rope and secured it. *Sally Ann* came to a halt and then began to move again as she was towed upriver by the rescue boat away from the dangerous weir.

Mia and Bibi were safe!

Kim felt a surge of triumph. She turned and flew tiredly back towards the woods. Flame sat waiting for her at the base of a birch tree, his little face turned up as he watched her intently.

Just then a large brown shape appeared in the sky above the wood.

Kim glimpsed its enormous yellow eyes and sharp curved talons.

It was another, much larger hawk. And it had spotted Flame.

Kim felt a stir of fear as she realized Flame was still watching her and hadn't noticed the danger he was in.

Kim didn't hesitate. She folded back her tired wings and went into a steep dive. Air whistled past her feathers as she gained on the other hawk. Gathering every last bit of strength, she slammed into the bird's side.

Brown feathers flew out everywhere. The larger hawk gave a loud screech of surprise and soared away.

'Oh!' Kim gasped, winded by the impact. She felt herself spinning downwards, out of control. The ground rushed up to meet her.

She closed her eyes, preparing for a horribly painful landing, when suddenly her trainers hit soft grass. Trainers! She was a girl again! Kim rolled over and over and then sat up, surprised to find that she was unhurt.

Flame ran towards her and leapt straight into her arms. 'You saved me, Kim. That took great courage. Thank you! You were very brave,' he purred loudly.

'I'm not really. I just couldn't bear it

if you were hurt,' Kim said, hugging him. A huge bubble of happiness seemed to swell inside her chest. 'I love having you as my friend, Flame. Please stay forever!'

Flame's eyes narrowed with affection. 'I will stay as long as I can,' he told her in a soft miaow that held a note of sadness.

'. . . And I still can't understand why you untied that rope. It was a very stupid thing to do. You could have drowned. How were we supposed to explain that to your mum and dad?' Kim's dad finished saying to Mia that evening.

Mia was hunched miserably on the sofa.

Looking at her cousin's face, Kim couldn't help feeling a bit sorry for her.

Mia had been really stupid, but Kim's mum and dad had just given her a telling-off she wouldn't forget in a hurry.

'I'm sorry, Uncle Brian. I didn't mean to cause so much trouble. Are . . . are you going to tell my mum and dad what happened?' Mia asked in a very small shaky voice.

Mrs Taylor put her arm round Mia's shoulders. 'Let's not worry about that, just now. No harm's done. Thank goodness the person in that motor boat realized you were in trouble.'

Mia nodded. 'Thanks, Aunt Joan. I'm really sorry,' she repeated.

Kim sat in silence. She really wished she could tell Mia about being turned into a hawk and how Flame's magic had saved her, but she knew she could never tell anyone Flame's secret.

Mr Taylor had calmed down now. 'Why don't you and Kim go and check on those chicks,' he said kindly to Mia.

Mia jumped up, eager to escape. 'Are you coming, Kim?'

Kim nodded. She and Mia dashed up the stairs. 'Phew! You really got roasted!' Kim said.

Mia shrugged. 'It could have been worse. Anyway, I deserved it.'

Kim was impressed. Mia hadn't tried to wriggle out of taking the blame for something she'd done this time. Maybe her cousin had turned over a new leaf.

As they went into her bedroom, Kim suddenly realized she hadn't seen Bibi for a while. She asked Mia about it.

'She kept miaowing to go into the garden, so I let her out. She's usually dead lazy. I don't know what she's interested in out there,' Mia told her.

Kim focused the telescope on the shed window. She saw the nest and the five chicks. They were getting really big now, with tiny wing feathers and stubby tails. She reckoned they'd be ready to leave the nest in a day or two.

'Aargh!' Kim almost jumped out of her skin.

Two big orange circles completely filled the eyepiece and blocked her view of the nest. Suddenly she realized what she was seeing.

'It's Bibi! She's inside the shed!' Kim gasped.

★Chapter★
SEVEN

Kim dashed after Mia as her cousin raced out of the room and pounded down the stairs.

Mia ran across the lawn at top speed and yanked open the shed door. 'Bibi! Don't you dare go near those chicks!' she warned, grabbing the big Persian.

Bibi howled with surprise and anger. Kim saw her wriggle free and

hurtle blindly out of the shed –
straight for a nearby bucket, which
tipped over and spilt smelly brown
liquid all over her.

By now Mia had checked that all the
chicks were fine. She gave a thumbs-up
sign to Kim, before going across to
Bibi.

Kim gave a huge sigh of relief.

'You bad girl! Look at the mess you're in!' Mia scolded. 'What is that horrible pongy stuff Bibi's covered in?'

'It's Dad's plant food. He makes it from nettles and sheep droppings!' Kim sputtered, trying not to laugh.

'Right! You're having a bath,' Mia said firmly. Holding Bibi at arm's length, she marched back into the house.

Kim suddenly realized that Flame hadn't followed her into the garden. That was odd. He usually came everywhere with her.

She found him still in the bedroom. He had crawled under her pillow and just his little tail was visible. When she uncovered him, he looked up at her with wide, troubled eyes.

'My enemies . . .' he told Kim in a scared little miaow.

Kim felt her chest tighten as she stroked him gently. 'Are . . . are they close?'

Flame shook his head. 'Not yet. But I can sense them.'

Kim didn't even want to think about what that could mean. 'We'll have to be very careful to keep you hidden then, won't we?' she said fiercely.

Flame seemed to relax a little and even began purring as she tickled him under the chin.

Just then Mia's complaining voice floated into the bedroom. 'Stop wriggling, Bibi! It's your own fault you're all sticky. You're getting a bath and that's that!'

Flame's purr turned into a chuckle. 'It
seems baths are not Bibi's favourite
thing!'

As Bibi gave another pitiful howl,
Kim couldn't help laughing too. 'I'd
better go and see if Mia needs some
help!'

Remembering how sharp Bibi's claws were, Kim borrowed her dad's thick gardening gloves. She held the squirming, hissing cat while Mia squirted her with pet cleaner and showered her. By the time Bibi was rinsed clean, Kim and Mia were soaked through. Bibi only settled down after Mia had dried her with a hairdryer and brushed her.

'There you are. You look beautiful,' Mia said, admiring Bibi's long, silky fur.

Kim changed into dry clothes. Helping to bath Bibi had been exhausting, but it was a small price to pay for saving the chicks. She was glad she and Mia seemed to be getting on better at last too.

'I'm glad you haven't got long fur!'

she said to Flame affectionately as he curled up in her room.

Flame wrinkled his nose. 'So am I. I hate baths too!'

It rained heavily the following day. Sullen grey clouds hung in the sky. Mia and Kim went for a morning walk, but it was too wet to be outdoors for long even with umbrellas and wellies. Flame and Bibi hated the rain and spent most of the time dozing in the bedrooms.

'What shall we do now?' Mia asked when they got home.

Kim didn't fancy reading or watching TV. 'We could make some cat toys. Mum's got loads of spare knitting wool,' she suggested.

She showed Mia how to wrap the
wool round card to make pompoms.
The toys turned out really well, but
Bibi wasn't too impressed when she
saw hers. She opened one eye to look
at it and then went straight back to
sleep.

Flame loved his toy. He seemed more
like his old self and not as nervous as
the day before. Kim and Mia played
with him for ages. Flame was so funny,
flattening his ears and play-growling as
he attacked the pompom on its length
of wool.

The phone rang and Kim went to
answer it. It was Granddad.

'Hi, Granddad. How are you?' Kim
said brightly. She told him about the
cat toys.

'It sounds like you and Mia are having fun,' he said with a chuckle. 'That's a really cute kitten you've got there. Tell your mum you're all invited over here tomorrow. Come straight on down to the jetty. I've got a surprise for you,' he said mysteriously.

'OK. See you tomorrow, Granddad.' Kim put down the phone and went to pass on the news. *I wonder what Granddad's up to*, she thought.

As she came back into the sitting room, a shaft of sunlight poured through the window. Kim saw that the garden was bright and fresh after the rain. Trailing the wool behind her, so that Flame chased after it, she went upstairs to check on the chicks.

As Kim focused on the hole in the shed, she saw a fat little bird perched there. It had speckled brown feathers, a fawn-coloured chest and yellow marks at the sides of its beak.

It was one of the chicks!

Kim watched with delight as the baby robin flapped its wings. Gaining confidence, it fluttered out and swooped across to the nearby apple tree.

Kim whirled round. 'Mia!' she shouted. 'Come quickly! The chicks are leaving the nest!'

Mia came running upstairs and into the bedroom.

'Take a look! There's another one at the hole!' Kim told her excitedly. 'It's getting ready to fly off!'

Mia saw the second robin make it safely into the apple tree, then she and Kim settled down to watch as two more babies flew out of the nest.

'Only one to go,' Kim said.

The last baby poked its head out of
the hole. It perched there, swaying
slightly, its feathers ruffled by the
breeze.

'It's a lot smaller than the others,' Mia
said. 'I hope it'll be OK.'

The baby robin didn't move.
Opening its beak, it gave a little chirp.
There was a flash of red as an adult
robin flew on to the shed roof.

Kim pointed a finger. 'It's one of the
parents. Look, it's trying to encourage
its baby to fly.'

Kim and Mia watched anxiously as
the baby robin fluttered straight down
to the lawn. It lay on the grass with its
tiny wings outspread and then flew
clumsily up to join the others in the
apple tree.

'Yes!' Kim yelled in relief. She grabbed Mia and they did a little dance of joy round the room.

★Chapter★
EIGHT

Kim's curiosity about Granddad's secret grew stronger when she saw the cheerful bunting strung between the trees on the way through the woods.

'I bet Gran and Granddad have finished work on the *Sally Ann*!' she whispered to Flame. 'Maybe we're all going on her maiden voyage.'

'What is that?' Flame seemed puzzled.

'It's when a new boat goes on her first trip,' Kim explained.

Gran and Granddad were already down at the small jetty when Kim and Flame, Mia and Bibi and Kim's parents arrived at the riverbank.

'Hello, everyone!' Granddad came out of the cabin to welcome them. He had a bottle of champagne in his hand. 'The great day is here at last! Our dear old boat is shipshape and ready to go!'

Sally Ann looked wonderful with her smart paint, gleaming brass rails and new red window boxes. Gran had draped a colourful shawl over her bow to cover the houseboat's name. Big bunches of balloons had been tied to the cabin. They bobbed about cheerfully in the river breeze.

Kim felt excited. This was like a birthday party for the houseboat.

Granddad came and stood next to Kim. 'I want you all to join with me as we celebrate the . . .' He gave a nod to his wife. Gran pulled the shawl away. '. . . *Sally Kim*'s first voyage!'

'Sally Kim? But . . .' Kim frowned. She thought Granddad had got the name wrong until she saw the bright new name painted on the bow.

Sally Ann had become the *Sally Kim*!

'Oh, Granddad! That's brilliant!' Kim said with a broad grin. She threw her arms around him for a huge hug.

'Well, an old boat can't have a proper maiden voyage, can she?' he said with a chuckle. 'So we gave her a different name and now she's a brand-new boat!'

Everyone clapped and cheered. They all piled on board and then Gran produced the bottle of champagne. Kim and Mia toasted the *Sally Kim* with glasses of lemonade.

There was a cake too, with red and blue candles. Gran had made a clever picture of the *Sally Kim* in icing. It even had a tiny porthole window, just like the real boat.

Gran lit the candles and Kim and
Mia blew them out.

'Did you make a wish?' Mia asked.

Kim looked at Flame, who was
sniffing the candle smoke-filled air
suspiciously. 'It's a secret.' She had
wished that she and Flame would share
lots and lots of trips on the *Sally Kim*.

'Isn't this fantastic!' Kim said to
Flame, around a mouthful of Gran's
delicious cake. 'I bet not many girls
have a boat named after them!'

Flame miaowed in agreement.

Granddad went forward to start the engine. 'This is the big moment!'

Kim held her breath. There was a tiny squeak, then a little rumble, and *Sally Kim* began chugging away from the jetty.

Kim and Mia cheered as *Sally Kim* made her way upriver and then fell about laughing as Kim's dad and granddad started singing together, 'Oh! A life on the ocean waves . . .'

They soon reached a quiet stretch of the river, where willow trees and reeds grew more thickly, hiding the bank from view.

'Do you want to have a go at steering?' Granddad asked Kim.

'I'll try,' Kim said. But she found it wasn't as easy as it looked. If she turned the wheel too far *Sally Kim* went towards the bank. When she tried to straighten her up, she turned the wheel too far the other way.

Poor *Sally Kim* chugged along in a very wobbly line!

'Oo-er!' Kim said, laughing helplessly. 'I'm rubbish at this! Do you want to try, Mia?'

'I don't mind.' Mia took the wheel. She frowned in concentration as she looked through the cabin window. The *Sally Kim* glided along smoothly in a perfect straight line.

'Gently does it,' Granddad coaxed.

'You're a natural, Mia!' Kim said admiringly.

Mia smiled, blushing with pleasure. 'I'm not bad.'

'Not bad?' Granddad patted Mia on the shoulder. 'She's quite the expert!'

'I'll leave you two to it!' Kim said with a grin.

She decided to take Flame and go through to the front of the boat, where there was a small sun deck with padded seats.

Kim's parents and gran sat at the tiny table, chatting over cups of tea and biscuits. They looked up and smiled as Kim pushed through the bead curtain in the open doorway and stepped down on to the small deck.

Kim patted a cushion and Flame settled beside her. She noticed that the clumps of weed here were very thick.

They grew right out from the bank, making the river seem narrow and a bit mysterious.

Kim stroked Flame's small velvety ears. 'How do you like it on the *Sally Kim*?'

'I like it very much,' Flame told her with a contented purr.

Kim had never felt so happy. She thought of the wish she had made when blowing out the candles. 'We are going to have loads of brilliant river trips with my grandparents and . . .' she began, and then stopped as Flame stiffened and suddenly sat bolt upright. 'What's wrong?' she asked him.

He had the same look on his face as when he had been hiding under her pillow.

Flame whined anxiously. The fur
along his back stood up in a ridge as
he stared fixedly at a thick clump of
rushes. There was movement in them,
as if something was pushing its way
through. Kim thought she heard a low,
powerful growl.

She felt the hairs on the back of her
neck prickle.

'My enemies are very close!' Flame
whimpered. 'I must go now!'

'Now?' Kim echoed in a tiny

quavering voice. This couldn't be happening. She really didn't think she could say goodbye to Flame yet.

Beside her, Flame was shaking with terror.

Kim had a horrible sinking feeling in her stomach at the thought of losing him. But it was far worse to think of Flame being killed. She knew she had to be strong.

'Go, Flame. Go, right now! Don't let them catch you!' she forced herself to say.

Sparks began glinting in Flame's fur and his whiskers crackled with magic.

Tears stung Kim's eyes. Suddenly she knew she couldn't bear to watch her friend leave. Turning round, she stumbled towards the beaded curtain, but forgot about the step and tripped.

Kim screamed as she grabbed at thin air. She hit the river with a splash. Icy-cold water closed over her head.

★Chapter★
NINE

Gasping and thrashing about, Kim surfaced. She tried to swim, but her soaked jeans and trainers made it difficult.

The *Sally Kim* was still heading away from her, upriver.

'Help!' she burbled, spitting out muddy water. 'He-elp!'

She saw her mum and dad and her

gran come out of the cabin. They waved frantically to her. 'Kim! Try and stay afloat! I'll throw you a rope!' yelled her dad.

Kim fought to stay calm. She was shivering and she could hardly feel her hands and feet.

She heard the *Sally Kim*'s engine go into reverse. The houseboat moved slowly backwards, her engine churning up the water.

Kim felt herself sinking and tried to kick out, but she could hardly move her legs. Something was wrapped round them. It must be waterweed. However much she tried to kick free, her legs were held fast by long tangled stems.

Kim started to panic as she sank under. In her mind she called out to Flame to help her, then remembered it was useless.

He had fled from his enemies. Flame was gone. No one could help her now.

She sank down and down.

Suddenly Kim felt something nudge against her shoulder. She turned round and found herself staring into an anxious pair of emerald eyes.

It was Flame! He had come back to save her.

Opening his little mouth Flame blew out an enormous sparkly air bubble. Kim felt the bubble brush softly against her cheek and then enclose her head, just like an old-fashioned diver's helmet.

She took a deep, shaky breath of air and forced herself to relax.

Through the clear bubble, she could see the jungle of weed and the river bottom just below her. Shoals of little fish were darting in all directions.

Flame waved a silver tabby paw to get her attention and then pointed towards the weed that was wound tightly round her legs.

Kim nodded to show that she understood. Flame began chewing the tough weed with his sharp teeth. Kim felt one leg come free and then the other one.

She began to kick out and under Flame's watchful eye rose slowly upwards.

As soon as Kim's head broke the surface, the air bubble popped. She half swam, half crawled through the muddy reed bed to reach the safety of the riverbank.

Kim pulled herself up on to the bank

and looked urgently round for any sign
of Flame. She caught a glimpse of his
soaked little form slipping out of the
river before there was a bright flash.
Kim saw Flame as a young white lion
once more, his coat glowing with
bright sparks. Next to him stood an old
grey lion with a kind, wise face. And
then Kim knew that it was now time
for Flame to go.

'Goodbye, Flame. Thank you for
saving me. I'll never forget you!' she
whispered.

For a second, her eyes and Flame's
eyes locked. 'Be well, Kim,' Flame
growled softly.

Then two slim, dark shapes broke
cover. Growling fiercely, Ebony's spies
ran straight at Flame.

Kim's blood ran cold. But Flame and the wise older lion had gone. Kim heard a faint howl of rage before the spies disappeared too.

She shivered and her heart felt like it was breaking, but Kim felt a sense of deep relief that Flame was safe.

'Kim! Kim! Are you all right?' shouted voices. Kim turned round and saw her parents as the *Sally Kim* drew up to the bank.

Everyone fussed over her, wrapping her in warm blankets and giving her hot drinks.

Mia threw her arms round Kim and hugged her tightly. 'I was so scared you'd drown!' she said tearfully and then she looked around. 'Where's Flame? We can't find him on the *Sally Kim*. He's . . . he's not . . .'

'Drowned?' Kim said, thinking quickly. 'No . . . I . . . I saw him get scooped up in a fishing net, by some fishermen in a boat.'

'Don't worry about Flame now, love,' her mum said. 'We'll have a proper look for him later. Let's get you out of these wet clothes . . .'

Kim nodded, knowing full well that they would never find Flame. She felt tired and sad, but her heart swelled with pride. A magic kitten had chosen her to be his friend. And she would always treasure the fond memories of Flame and their adventure together.

She linked hands with Mia, who smiled warmly at her. The rest of the school holidays stretched out before them.

Flame's Favourites

1. Snoozing – I love cuddling up with a friendly young two-legs.

2. My favourite food to gobble up is – well, I'm spoiled for choice – bits of cheese, sardine sandwiches, scrambled eggs. But best of all is kitty food from a packet. Crunchy-munchy – yummy!

3. Going out with a dear two-legs friend is such fun. Your world is so busy and colourful. Riding on buses and looking out of the window is epic!

4. Playing with shiny things tied to the ends of sticks, chasing scrunched-up crisp-packet balls, darting after cat-nip toys – oh, I could do that all day!

5. I love grooming my fur, washing my face and nibbling at the tickly bits between my toes – that always make me giggle.

6. Racing around with other animals, tumbling about and nipping each other's fur is brilliant. Unless you get a mouthful of muddy, smelly dog!

7. Having a bath is loads of fun – with lots and lots of foamy bubbles to pat with my paws. But the water must be lovely and warm, and not too deep.

8. Having my wet fur dried with a hand-held, hot-air blowy thing feels so good and it makes me into a total fluff-ball!

9. I love being rubbed under my chin and on the top of my head as much as I enjoy having my ears stroked.

10. Investigating small spaces and seeing if I can squeeze inside is a great way to pass the time. Under cupboards is good. Inside cupboards is even better.

Crisscross Challenge

Follow the clues to complete this
Flame-themed crossword.

ACROSS

1.   Cats and dogs are popular _ _ _ _.
4.   The name for a group of kittens.
6.   When Flame appears as a lion he is this colour.
7.   Flame is the _ _ _ _ _ _ Kitten.
8.   The name of Flame's uncle.
10. Flame's uncle rules the Lion _ _ _ _ _ _ _ _.
12. The old grey lion who protects Flame.
13. Lion cubs are born and live here.

DOWN
2. Flame has _____-green eyes.
3. An angry cat might hiss and ____.
5. Flame dreams of taking his place on the Lion _____.
6. These bristles on Flame's face crackle with magic.
9. Flame has royal _____.
11. A cat uses this to smell.

Answers on the last page.

Corny Cat Jokes

What is a cat's favourite colour?

Purrrrrrple.

What do cats eat for breakfast?

Mice Krispies.

What is a cat's favourite film?

The Sound of Mewsic.

What do you call a cat that eats a duck?

A duck-filled fatty puss.

What happened when the cat swallowed a ball of wool?

She had mittens.

What do you use to comb a cat?

A catacomb.

Star Dreams

Jemma's biggest dreams become
possible when she discovers silky
cream-and-brown kitten Flame...

Answers

Crisscross Challenge

Across:
1. Pets   4. Litter   6. White
7. Magic   8. Ebony   10. Kingdom
12. Cirrus   13. Den

Down:
2. Emerald   3. Spit   5. Throne
6. Whiskers   9. Blood   11. Nose

For lots more Magic Kitten fun, visit

www.puffin.co.uk/suebentley